A Christmas Pageant for JESUS

Celebrating God's GRACE

by Susan Jones

Illustrated by Lee Holland

Good Books

New York, New York

As the bright sun rises,
Little Chipmunk pops his head
out of his tree. It's a special day!

"I'm ready, Mama!" Little Chipmunk exclaims.

"Of course you are," Mama chuckles. "I'm excited for your first Christmas pageant, too."

As they scurry on their way,
Little Chipmunk dreams about
his big moment in the pageant.

"There you are!"
calls Little Bunny.

Celebrating

"Is everyone ready to begin?"
calls Badger.

And with a hush, things quiet
down, and Little Chipmunk
remembers something.

He's forgotten baby Jesus at home!
The manger will be empty and it
will be all his *fault!*

It's too far to journey home and back in time.

What now—a Christmas pageant without Jesus?!

"It's almost our turn," whispers
Little Bunny excitedly.

But Little Chipmunk isn't there to hear.

Little Chipmunk feels so alone. Surely this is the worst thing to ever happen at Christmas.

Soon, two kind eyes
peer back at him.

"Why did you run off?"
asks Mama, gently.

"I left Jesus behind," Little Chipmunk cries. "I've ruined everything!"

"Little Chipmunk, Jesus is always with us. He knows we're not perfect," says Mama.

"And He knows what we *feel* because He came to Earth as a baby."

"Let's pray that this pageant will simply make Jesus smile," encourages Mama.

As they walk back to the pageant, Little Chipmunk spots an unusual stone.

"I have an *idea*," he says.

The *forest friends* spot Little
Chipmunk and Mama returning.

"We were so worried!" Little Bunny
says, rushing to them.

"Did we miss the end of the pageant?"
Little Chipmunk asks.

"Of course not! When we saw you
were missing, we stopped and prayed,"
Little Bunny says.

"Do you have Jesus to place in the manger?" Badger asks.

"We always have Jesus with us," says Little Chipmunk.

"But this will help us remember."

"I know this pageant made Jesus smile," Little Chipmunk whispers to Mama.

"How do you know?" asks Mama with a wink.

"Because it was all a gift of love for Jesus, just like He gave to us," Little Chipmunk beams.

Good Books books may be purchased in bulk at special discounts for sales promotion, corporate gifts, fund-raising, or educational purposes. Special editions can also be created to specifications. For details, contact the Special Sales Department, Good Books, 307 West 36th Street, 11th Floor, New York, NY 10018 or info@skyhorsepublishing.com.

Good Books is an imprint of Skyhorse Publishing, Inc.®, a Delaware corporation.

Visit our website at www.goodbooks.com.

10 9 8 7 6 5 4 3 2 1

Library of Congress Cataloging-in-Publication Data is available on file.

Cover design by Katie Jennings Campbell
Cover and interior illustration by Lee Holland

Print ISBN: 978-1-68099-540-4
Ebook ISBN: 978-1-68099-551-0

Printed in China